NO!

David McPhail

Roaring Brook Press New York

For teachers everywhere.

Published by Roaring Brook Press
Roaring Brook Press is a division of Holtzbrinck Publishing Holdings Limited Partnership
175 Fifth Avenue, New York, New York 10010

Distributed in Canada by H. B. Fenn and Company Ltd.

Cataloging-in-Publication Data is on file at the Library of Congress
ISBN-10: 1-59643-288-8
ISBN-13: 978-1-59643-288-8

Roaring Brook Press books are available for special promotions and premiums.
For details contact: Director of Special Markets, Holtzbrinck Publishers.

First Edition March 2009
Printed in China
10 9 8 7 6 5 4 3 2 1